Enjoy a SNEAK PR

D0285726

SPEED DATING
by Nancy Warren

February 2007

Ultrasensible Kendall Clarke—the shining star of number crunchers—posing as the girlfriend of celebrity NASCAR driver Dylan Hargreave? It seems she's assessed the risk and she's taking it!

THUNDERSTRUCK
by Roxanne St. Claire

February 2007

Mick Churchill knew buying out half of Shelby Jackson's family-owned race team was going to be tricky. The struggling team needs Mick's media savvy and team-building skills—even if Shelby can't admit it. Now, with Daytona just days away, Mick won't quit until he changes Shelby's mind.

HEARTS UNDER CAUTION
by Gina Wilkins

February 2007

One minute Lisa Woodrow is a big-city prosecutor, and the next she's back home, hiding out from an escaped convict. Suddenly, staying beneath the radar in North Carolina doesn't seem to be such a bad idea, especially when she finds herself under the protection of her ex-fiancé, crew chief Wade McClellan....

Look for a valuable coupon offer inside!

ISBN-13: 978-0-373-15099 1
ISBN-10:   0-373-15099 7

CONTENTS

HARLEQUIN

Driver cameo:
Carl Edwards

///// **NASCAR**

SPEED DATING
Nancy Warren
USA TODAY bestselling author

CHAPTER ONE

KENDALL CLARKE was looking forward to the most exciting night of her life.

Only thirty-one years old, she would be the youngest recipient of the prestigious Sharpened Pencil Award for being chosen Actuary of the Year.

For the hundredth time, she tracked across the carpet of her hotel room in Charlotte, North Carolina, to practice the acceptance speech she'd give tonight at the closing banquet of the actuarial association dinner. She wanted to come across as humbled to be receiving this great honor, but also proud of the work done by her company.

"Ladies and gentlemen, colleagues, friends." She paused as she'd been taught in the public speaking refresher course she'd taken the second she learned she'd be making this speech.

Breathe, she reminded herself. *Look out at the audience. Smile.* "Trust is the cornerstone of our business," she informed the blue-upholstered chair in the corner of the room. She put an emphasis on *trust.* Such a nice, strong word to start a speech with. *Trust.*

There was an hour or so before she needed to head down to ballrooms A and B, where the American Association of Actuaries was holding its annual conference and awards banquet. She'd sent her dress down for pressing earlier in the day, wanting everything to be perfect. She bit her lip. The dress ought to be back.

Willing to leave nothing to chance, she called down to Housekeeping. After many a long, lonely ring of the phone, a hesitant female voice said, *"Hola?"*

It didn't take Kendall long to realize that the woman spoke almost no English, and Kendall's Spanish wasn't any better. She thought after a few minutes of labored conversation that she'd got her request through. She wanted them to hurry up with her dress and send it to her room.

She'd barely replaced the receiver in its cradle when it rang.

"Kendall Clarke," she said at her most formal, because you never knew at a business conference who might be calling. But, as she'd hoped, the voice at the other end belonged to Marvin Fulford, her colleague and fiancé.

"Kendall, it's me, Marvin," he said. He was so sweet. They never shared a room when traveling because both agreed it gave the wrong impression. Indeed, this time Marvin had gone so far as to book a room on a different floor.

"Hi, Marvin. Are you going to pick me up here so we can arrive at the banquet together?" That was one of the perks of working with your fiancé, she'd long thought. She rarely had to attend big business events alone.

"Um, I was hoping to come up now and talk to you for a few minutes."

He sounded odd. As if he was nervous. Probably on her behalf. "Great. I can practice my speech on a real person. Come right up."

Or maybe, she thought, as she replaced the phone, he wanted to make love before the ceremony. Her pulse quickened. What a wonderful way to relax before her big moment. Their sex life had been sparse to nonexistent lately, so the idea of him wanting to jump her bones right before the banquet filled her with delight.

She'd planned to surprise him with some sexy new lingerie she'd bought—well, sexy for her. Her makeup, hair and nails were all done, courtesy of the hotel salon, so it took her no time at all to slip into the black demi bra and high-cut panties and the black silk slip she'd bought at Victoria's Secret. Her black stockings were sheer as a whisper and her black sandals were strappy, with a low but shapely heel. She'd debated stilettos but you didn't work in the actuary business without learning a lot of very useful facts, like the stats on back pain and injury stemming from the wearing of high-heeled shoes. Besides, she didn't want to stumble on the way to the stage. Not in front of all her professional colleagues.

She was tingling with anticipation when a knock sounded on her door. Of course, they wouldn't have a lot of time, but with Marvin not a lot of time was necessary. Oh, well. Once they were married and things settled down, they could spend more time on the intimate part of their relationship.

She struck a sultry pose, then felt ridiculous,

so she simply reminded herself to stand up straight, then opened the door.

Marvin stood on the other side wearing khakis and a golf shirt. The fact that he wasn't yet dressed for the banquet made her very glad she'd slipped into her sexy underwear.

But Marvin didn't even seem to notice. He glanced up and down the hall before he entered her room, looking furtive and not remotely like a man bent on a prebanquet quickie.

"Marvin? Is everything all right?" She'd wondered if he was a little jealous that she'd received this honor instead of him. Surely he could be happy for her, as she'd have been for him. They were planning to spend their lives together. Wasn't a marriage all about mutual respect, compatibility and support?

"I have something to tell you, Kendall, that may shock you," he said, glancing up and then away. His pale blond hair was shorter than usual, she noted. He must have had a trim. He'd never be confused with Brad Pitt, but he was a pleasant-looking man, she thought. Maybe a little on the pale side, but he did suffer from asthma.

She smiled at him. "Is it good news?" This was

the kind of conference where networking was abundant. Had he been offered a job of some kind?

"Good news?" He glanced at her again, as though surprised by the question. Then, as was typical of him, he took a moment to ponder. Marvin always looked at all sides of a question. It was a quality she admired in him.

"In some ways it is good news. Very good news," he said. "But *you* may not think so."

"It's a job offer, isn't it? Is it very far away from Portland?" The possibility had always existed that one of them would get a better offer elsewhere. They'd never discussed what they'd do in that eventuality. Did she have to be tested now? Couldn't Marvin have waited until after the banquet?

"No. It's not a job offer. It's…" He blew out a breath. "It's personal. I don't know how to begin."

The first icy claws of apprehension scratched the surface of her happiness. "Personal?"

"I never meant to hurt you, Kendall. I swear. The whole thing was…unplanned."

"What whole thing?" she asked, feeling a numbness start to creep into her toes.

Marvin's pale cheeks took on a faint pink

hue and he looked everywhere but at her. She'd never seen him so uncomfortable.

"I've fallen in love," he said at last. "With someone else."

She blinked. Opened her mouth and then closed it again.

When she didn't speak, he went on. "I never meant for it to happen. To hurt you. Behind your back. I don't know what I was thinking. I wanted to tell you, but I didn't know how. I…"

"You're in love with someone else?" she repeated stupidly.

"Yes."

"But we've interviewed caterers, picked out china. We're on the third draft of our guest list…"

He was rubbing a spot on the carpet with the toe of his brown tasseled loafer, giving the nub of worsted his full attention. After she petered out, there was a moment of painful silence.

"Who is it? This person you've fallen in love with." Her voice was calm, for which she'd always be grateful.

"Penelope Varsan." He made eye contact and then his gaze slid away.

Kendall stared at him. "Our colleague?

You've been seeing a woman we both work with behind my back?"

"It was an accident. I swear. We were both working late night after night on the Wayman file and…one thing led to another. I didn't know how to tell you. I'm sorry."

"Why are you telling me now?" She raised a hand to her head. "I can't even think. I'm supposed to give a speech and all I'll be able to concentrate on is that my date for the evening is in love with another woman."

"Well, um, that's why I wanted to tell you now. You see…" He sighed heavily and sat down in the wing chair beside the small table where she'd set up her laptop. "Penelope's going to have a child."

"She's pregnant?" Kendall's voice was barely a whisper.

"Yes."

"Then this must have been going on for months."

"About four months."

"Oh, Marvin. How could you betray me like that?"

"I wanted to wait until after this conference to tell you. You must have felt that things haven't been close between us for some time."

She snorted. "Now I know why."

"I like and respect you, Kendall. You have a fine mind and you're an excellent actuary. I mistook professional respect for…warmer feelings."

"What are you saying?" All her life she'd searched for the one person who would love her forever. A man like her father, who'd be faithful and true to his family. She wasn't looking for fireworks and matinee-idol, multi-millionaire hotshots. All she'd ever wanted was a steady, decent man who'd love her and any family they might have. She'd aimed so low, and still she'd failed. Somehow she needed to understand why.

"You're a wonderful person, but you're not… Well, Penelope's exciting. She's passionate. I realized that's what was missing with us."

Her leaden stomach grew heavier. "So, I'm not exciting enough for you?"

"It's not your fault, Kendall. I need more."

"Well, I guess you're getting it." She rubbed her forehead. "I can't believe this."

"As you may know, when women are in a delicate situation, they can become quite emotional."

"Thank you for the prenatal lesson, Marvin."

"The thing is, Penelope's feeling very insecure and it's making her a bit clingy."

"What is your point?"

"She wants me to sit with her at the banquet tonight. That's why I had to tell you right away. I would, of course, have said no. I want to support you. This is a big night for you and for our firm, but she's carrying my child." He paused for a moment, and she could tell he was savoring the phrase. His narrow chest swelled a little. "I have to think of my family."

"So, you're dumping me. Just like that. Right before the biggest night of my life."

He smiled at her, obviously relieved to have the burden of his confession off his chest and no hysterics to wade through. "You're strong, Kendall. You don't need me the way Penelope does."

He walked to the door and opened it, then glanced back. "Good luck tonight." He sounded as though he really meant it.

After the door shut behind her ex-fiancé, Kendall stood there feeling frozen and numb. Bits of thoughts and phrases were jumbled up in her head. *Not exciting enough. Pregnant. I need more.*

And through it all flickered the humiliating knowledge that this relationship had gone on for months under her nose and she'd never noticed. She had the sick feeling that she was the only one in the office who hadn't.

This was supposed to be the night of her greatest triumph, not her greatest humiliation.

If only she could think more clearly.

She stood there in her new underwear and slowly tugged the engagement ring off her finger and regarded the diamond solitaire. Like her dreams, it was modest.

She ought to return it to Marvin, but he was just thrifty enough that he might offer the ring to Penelope.

She put the ring on the dresser where it made a tiny click. She'd leave it as a tip for the maid.

Having decided the ring's future to her satisfaction, she glanced at her clock and discovered with horror that the banquet was starting in fifteen minutes. Luckily she was ready. No, wait, she wasn't. Something was missing. She looked around vaguely.

Oh, of course. Her dress. The one Marvin had helped her pick out at Nordstrom.

DYLAN HARGREAVE gave a rebel yell into the headset, knowing he'd half deafen his spotter and any of the crew who were listening.

"She's sweet," he yelled, feeling the grab of the tires, the tightness of tail. He accelerated into Turn Three at the Speedway in Charlotte, pulling the wheel hard left, hanging on to control as he fought for more speed. A glance at the oversize tachometer told him the engine was cooperating.

Charlotte was his track. He always did well here. Being a North Carolina boy, it was important for him to place high in Sunday's race for a lot of reasons. Today's training run was feeling good. He was pumped; the team members were working together like magic.

The run of bad luck they'd suffered recently was about to end. He loved race week in Charlotte, culminating in the big race.

Sunday, he fully intended to take a victory lap.

He owned this course, and anybody who wanted to try and take him better be ready to do serious battle.

Then he felt the speed fall away as though somebody'd turned off the ignition.

"Aaaaw, no!" he yelled, as a multicolored blur of cars zoomed past him like a swarm of bees. It was only a practice to make sure everything was running smoothly, but it was clear that things on the Hargreave team weren't going smoothly at all.

After they'd towed the car into the huge garage, by the hauler that housed a second race car and all the tools and spare parts they might need, Mike Nugent, his crew chief, slapped him on the back. "Probably the fuel line, Dy. We'll get it fixed for Sunday."

Dylan nodded. He didn't bother saying anything. Every one of the glum faces on the team reflected his own expression. Luck. They really needed some luck.

Preferably the good kind.

As usual, even though it was only a practice, loads of fans were out, a number of them gorgeous young women. Dylan didn't quite know how the young women of America had suddenly decided stock car racing was sexy, but he wasn't complaining. To Dylan, they made his job a lot more interesting.

There was at least a vanload of college girls crowding him now as he made his way to the garage, but he didn't mind. They all had long hair and bare legs. Sure, the hair color was different, and some bared their legs with little bitty skirts, and some wore butt-hugging shorts, and unless he learned their names he'd have trouble telling them apart.

The blonde whose T-shirt read NASCAR CHICK told him her name was Tiffanny, with two *N*s. "Where y'all from, girls?" he asked as he obligingly autographed a ball cap with his number on it. Some women gave him a hard time for using terms like *girls,* but he wasn't going to stop. Political correctness was so complicated he'd pretty much given up trying to figure it out. He believed to the depth of his being that women should get paid the same money for the same work as men, that they could pretty much do anything they pleased. However, he also believed it was his God-given responsibility as a man to treat women with a little special courtesy, and if a young woman in a miniskirt wanted his autograph, then she might have to put up with him opening a door or pulling out her chair for her or calling her a girl.

"California," she said, all suntanned legs and long blond hair and not looking at all that offended he'd referred to her and her friends as girls.

"Long way from home."

"We came specially to see you," she said, as

she'd no doubt say to any other driver she could stop. "Are you going to win on Sunday?"

"Honey," he said, "I am going to do my very best."

Then he posed for a photo with the bunch of them and took the next item shoved under his nose. As he signed a copy of today's newspaper, he wondered idly how many dorm rooms had his picture tacked up on the wall and shrugged.

Who could figure celebrity?

He made sure all the kids in the vicinity got an autograph, and then with a final wave and a "thanks, folks," he walked past the guards and back into the garage where his crew was already crawling over his car like ants over picnic leftovers.

"Hey, Dy," Mike Nugent said. "Me and the crew are going for dinner and a couple beers tonight. You coming?"

"Can't. I'm going to a wedding."

"Who do you know getting married in Charlotte?" Mike asked.

"Ashlee."

The older man blinked slowly. "You're going to your ex-wife's wedding?"

"It's kind of a tradition. I've been to all of 'em."

He and Mike had known each other for years. His crew chief regarded him with eyes that had worked on metal chassis so long they'd taken on the color of steel. "Make sure you don't end up as the groom—again."

Ashlee, his ex, had gone on TV twice now claiming he and she were getting back together. Both times it had come as a big surprise to Dylan. Probably a bigger surprise to the poor sap she was set to marry tonight.

"I've got it covered."

"Why do you let her get away with this stuff?"

He thought about it. "Ashlee's trying to find a way to be happy. I wasn't much of a husband, so if she wants to have some fun at my expense once in a while, who am I to blame her?"

"Dy, buddy, she wants you back."

"Not going to happen."

CHAPTER TWO

KENDALL KNEW her disastrous day had sunk another notch when she accidentally locked herself out of her hotel room.

In her underwear.

Unable to believe she could have been so easily bested by a fire door, she tried the knob, pushed her hip against the door, but it remained sullenly closed.

Kendall wasn't the sort of person to walk out of a door without ensuring it stayed open for her safe return. Stress and shock, she discovered, could do strange things to a person. Added to the natural stress of being dumped by her fiancé on the very day she was to receive the greatest compliment of her career was the rising panic that she'd miss her moment of glory. She hadn't come all the way to Charlotte to accept the Sharpened Pencil Award in her underwear.

Embarrassment prickled along her skin as she stood there for a moment wondering what on earth to do. She'd only stepped outside to see if her dress was back yet.

Breathe, she told herself, determined not to panic. She was top-to-toe ready, so the minute the dress arrived—and she found someone to let her back into her hotel room—she'd grab her clutch purse and her neatly typed acceptance speech and go.

A minute ticked by. Two. The air felt overwarm and she heard the faint noises of a large building, but saw no sign of her dress. There was no hotel phone on her floor. Could she slide into the stairwell and creep downstairs, then somehow get a hotel employee's attention?

Yes, she thought. That's what she'd do. Tonight would be the culmination of her career and she couldn't be late—especially since her ex and his recently outed love would be sure to think she was moping. Her chin went up at the thought. She might have a broken heart, but she was hanging on to her pride with every ounce of willpower.

At last, the sound she'd been waiting for— the whir of the elevator and then the *clunk, shhhh* as it stopped at her floor. She jogged forward, anxious for clothing. Ahead of her, a room door opened and a man came out, luckily without looking her way, at the exact moment the elevator doors opened. Horror of horrors, over the man's solid shoulder she saw three of the regional managers from her company—including her own boss—step out.

Kendall didn't stop to think. In one smooth gesture—and a surprisingly quick one, thanks to the panic-driven adrenaline suddenly coursing through her veins—she stuck her hand out and caught the door the stranger had exited from before it closed.

Then she slipped inside the unknown man's room.

Even as she sagged in relief, having whisked herself out of sight before the trio of managers saw her, she knew what she was doing was wrong. Thankfully, this room door didn't seem to be as efficiently quick at slamming behind a person as her own, but that was no excuse for trespassing. Still, she only wanted to use his phone to call down to the front desk and get someone to track down her dress and another room key. And this time she wasn't giving up until she was certain her request had been understood.

She walked down the short hallway past the bathroom and closet into the main part of the room, idly noting a black case on a luggage stand and a pair of dirty socks on the floor. She averted her eyes as though that would minimize her rude intrusion into another guest's space.

Perhaps she should write the stranger a polite note explaining her behavior....

Or would it, in fact, show better manners if she—

Her etiquette dilemma ended when she got to the main room and found a man there. It had never occurred to her that there could be someone else inside. Before she could open her mouth to apologize, he glanced at her and said, "You're late. I'd about given up on you."

Kendall blinked stupidly as she looked up at a man who seemed vaguely familiar. Not another actuary. Something about his air of danger told her he didn't calculate risk for a living. He was only a couple of inches taller than she was in her heels, but muscled and hard-bodied. There was a scar on his cheek that seemed unnecessarily large—as though it was showing off what a tough guy he was.

"I'm so, so sorry," she stammered. "I would

never normally enter someone else's hotel room—"

"No problem. I'm glad Mike let you in. I was waiting for you. Come on, let's go." He looked her up and down in a way that suddenly reminded her she was still in her underwear. "Nice dress."

"It's a slip."

"Never can get the hang of ladies' fashion terms. Looks good on you. Sexy." He picked up a light gray suit jacket and pulled it on over matching slacks and a crisp white shirt, which clearly suggested somebody in this hotel got their clothes pressed in a timely manner. He wore no tie, but his black shoes shone.

Sexy? He thought she looked sexy? Some of her embarrassment at being caught in a slip faded. Okay, quite a bit.

He walked up to her and put an arm around her shoulders, turning her toward the door. At his touch she experienced the strangest sense of weakness. He had the kind of energy that could carry a person with it, whether she wanted to go or not.

When they got to the door, she realized she had to stop him or she'd be back where she started—out in that corridor with no clothes. She turned. "Um, just a second."

He reached around her for the door handle. The door at her back and Mr. Muscle in front was the absolute definition of being stuck between a rock and a hard place. His jacket just brushed her arm and as he looked down at her she noted his eyes were a deep, mossy green with brown-and-gold flecks. "What's your name?"

"Kendall Clarke," she said and foolishly stuck out her hand.

"Kendall. Do you go by Ken? Kenny? K.C.?" He spoke with the syrupy drawl that suggested he was from around these parts.

She shuddered. "I most certainly do not. It's Kendall."

Solemnly, he shook her hand. "Pleased to make your acquaintance." He didn't say ma'am, but the accent implied it. "You seem a little uptight there, Kendall. Everything all right?" The way he said her name, it sounded like Ken Doll.

"If I could use your phone?"

"No time. You can phone from my car. Come on."

"Your car?" She put a hand to her head, partly to see if it was still attached to her body. Too much had happened today. The tug of familiarity when she looked at him didn't help. "Who are you?" she finally asked.

Amusement flickered in his eyes, fascinating her. "I thought Bryce was going to fill you in. My name's Dylan. My friends call me Dy."

And thunk, it all fell into place like three cherries in a slot machine, although of course she'd never play a slot machine. You didn't have to be an actuary to figure out that the odds were stacked against the player.

That's why he'd seemed familiar. Dylan Hargreave was a NASCAR driver. And not just any driver. He'd caused the kind of sensation even a non sports buff like Kendall had noticed. "You're ranked fifteenth so far this season." It wasn't that she followed sports, but rankings and number systems of every kind appealed to her and sort of stuck in her brain. There were a lot of numbers stuck in there.

"Wait till Sunday, honey. All that will change. This speedway's my track." She felt his intensity like an engine revving. "Bryce said you were a fan."

"Bryce said that?" Whoever Bryce was.

"Sure. I promise tonight won't be too boring. We'll have dinner, make nice, and be on our way. We can catch up to Bryce after if you like."

She felt as if she were in a dream; everything was a little misty around the edges and didn't make any sense. "This is a date?"

His smile crinkled the corners of his eyes and made that scar turn from a wobbly *L* to a *C*. "You're right. It's not a date, exactly, more an acting job. I sure do appreciate you being able to make it."

She'd always thought Southern men had more than their fair share of charm, but this guy was in a league all his own.

NASCAR driver, Actuary of the Year, acting job. It wasn't adding up.

"Can you handle it?" This man regarded her from those mossy-green eyes as though she weren't the brightest spark. How extraordinary. She supposed he had ample reason to doubt her intelligence, given that she'd stumbled into his room half-dressed and seemed to echo every statement he made. For a few luscious moments, she was experiencing what it might feel like to be a silly woman. Not silly, she reminded herself. Sexy.

The kind of woman a virile and exciting man like this might look at twice.

He stared right into her eyes a moment longer and she took that as a good excuse to stare back. Rough, tough and gorgeous. His hair was a tumble of dark brown with the kind of streaky gold that suggested he spent time in the sun. His skin was weathered, the mouth uncompromising, the jaw cleft. And that scar fascinated her.

"I don't want to be rude, but do you really need Bryce to find you dinner dates?" The guy was great-looking, successful, rich. He didn't look like the sort of man to need help getting female companionship.

He scratched a spot behind his ear. "Bryce was supposed to explain all this. I needed an actress. You just hang all over me, pretend we're crazy in love. For a couple of hours at this wedding we're going to, I want people thinking I have a girlfriend. That's all."

"I'm to appear as your girlfriend without actually being one?"

"That's right. Can you handle it?"

She laughed at the bitter irony of her situation. "Oh, yes. I've had practice."

He glanced at a watch that looked designed

for a scuba diver rather than a race car driver. "We'd better get going."

Not much of an explanation, but she really didn't have time to get into this guy's relationships with women.

Now was the time to tell him that Bryce hadn't sent her, she was wearing a black silk slip from Victoria's Secret and that no one was ever going to mistake her for a NASCAR driver's girlfriend.

She was the kind of woman that the man she'd been dating for two years dumped on a business trip so he could sit at the actuary banquet with his pregnant girlfriend.

And suddenly the thought of slogging through dinner alone, while Marvin and Penelope canoodled in some dark corner, was simply too pathetic. Kendall had a secret romantic streak. She gobbled up novels and subscribed to a couple of movie channels including an oldies station. She loved the moment, especially in old films, when the enraged heroine slapped the out-of-line guy, when she stood up and said, "Nobody treats me this way."

Maybe all that reading and viewing hadn't

been a waste of her time, as she'd sometimes thought. Maybe it was training for her moment to stand up and slap Marvin—metaphorically, of course.

A thought struck, so utterly blinding in its brilliance and daring, that her heart jumped unpleasantly.

The NASCAR driver standing in front of her at this very minute believed she could pass as his girlfriend. Why on earth couldn't she see what that would be like?

On the heels of that thought came another, even more scintillating.

What if she showed up at her banquet with this walking shrine to testosterone? This man, she suddenly recalled, who'd been featured in *People*'s 50 Hottest Bachelors issue. Wouldn't that show Marvin—and everyone? Not exciting enough, huh?

What if she talked Dylan Hargreave into dropping by her awards dinner? The voice of reason that had stopped her doing anything crazy, or even remotely interesting, for the thirty-one years of her life, said in a snide, evil-stepmother voice in her ear, "In your unmentionables?"

She ignored the little snide voice. Not giving herself time to think this through, since, if she did, she'd do the sensible thing, she said, "I have an event myself I need to attend here in the hotel later on. Could we be back here by, say, ten?"

She was scheduled to receive her award after the dinner and speeches. The agenda said ten-fifteen, and based on her knowledge of previous awards dinners, the award would be presented precisely at the time indicated.

"Sure. It gives us an excuse to leave. What's your shindig?"

"I'm receiving an award," Kendall said, not without pride.

"Cool. An acting award?"

She ought to get one for this performance. She did her best to look enigmatic. "I'll explain later."

What was she doing? she asked herself again as they walked down the hall toward the elevator. There was no answer forthcoming. All she knew was that she liked the feeling that she could pass for the date of the Sexiest NASCAR Driver Alive. She felt his energy and laugh-in-the-face-of-danger personality beside her. That personality was so big and so strong she felt it spilling over and imbuing her with craziness. She had no purse, no room key, nothing. Not so much as a tissue. She'd never done anything this wild in her life. Oh, it felt good.

The elevator doors opened on a couple kissing so passionately the mirrored walls had steamed up. The man had pale blond hair and wore a suit. The woman wore something black and low cut at the back. Even before the man lifted his head, Kendall was tugging Dylan's big hand and turning for the stairs. She recognized that suit. She'd been with Marvin when he bought it in the January sales last year.

"Let's give them some privacy," she said in a low voice as she tugged.

"Kendall?" Marvin sounded like a man who couldn't believe his eyes. Jerk.

"You know that guy?" Dylan asked as the fire door shut them into the stairwell.

"No," she said. It was true. She'd never known Marvin, not all the time she'd dated him, helped him get ahead in the company. He'd seemed as dull as she was, which made him a safe risk. Or so she'd thought. As it had turned out, he was a bad risk, one she'd have to write off. As though her life were an insurance policy.

Her heels clicked defiantly as she ran down the stairs, echoing like hail while Dylan's heavier tread sounded like a drum.

By the time they'd clicked and drummed their way past the reception floor, she had to admit she had completely lost her mind. She wasn't getting off to go and pick up her dress and her room key, and she wasn't going to the awards banquet to sit meekly with the other onesies.

She was blowing off the banquet.

Predictable and safe hadn't worked out so well.

She wondered what wild would feel like.

She had a feeling she was about to find out.

* * * * *

Kendall usually keeps the brakes on, but she's assessed the risk with Dylan and she's taking it! Join Kendall in the fast lane in SPEED DATING *by Nancy Warren, on sale in February 2007 for a limited time. See next page for a valuable coupon.*

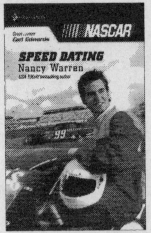

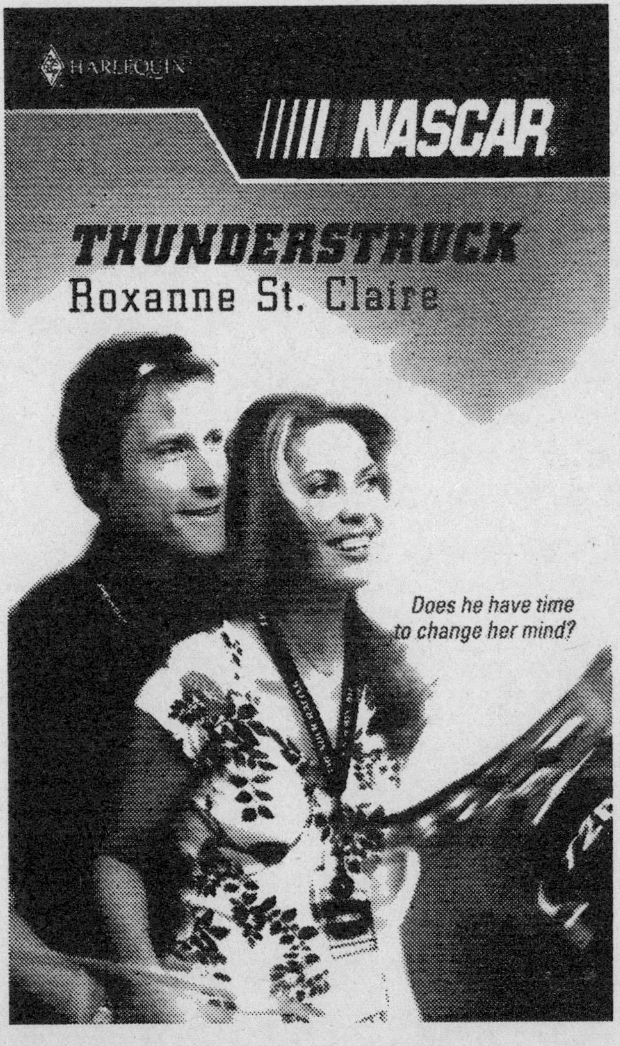
HARLEQUIN
NASCAR
THUNDERSTRUCK
Roxanne St. Claire
Does he have time
to change her mind?

CHAPTER ONE

SHELBY JACKSON STEPPED through the door of Thunder Racing and sucked in a lungful of her favorite scent—motor oil and gasoline, tinged with a hint of welding glue. No double espresso or honey-laden pastry could smell better in the morning. But there was something different in the air today. She sniffed again, drawn into the race shop by her nose and her sixth sense.

There was something pungent, a little bitter but…fresh. Her heart jumped and her work boots barely touched the gleaming white floor as she hurried toward the paint-and-body shop. With a solid shove, she flung the double doors, and they smacked the walls with a satisfying synchronized clunk.

And then she drank in the prettiest sight she'd seen in eight long years.

Number fifty-three lived again.

"Oh, Daddy," she whispered as she approached the race car, the hand over her mouth barely containing her delight. "You'd love it."

In truth, Thunder Jackson would roar like an eight-hundred-horsepower engine at the sight of the screaming-yellow "fifty-three" surrounded by a sea of purple as painful as a fresh black eye. Then he'd calm down and throw his arm around her shoulder with a mile-wide grin and a gleam of approval in his eyes.

"Shelby girl," that gravelly voice would say. "You done good."

And she had.

She took a few steps closer, nearly reaching the driver's side. The Kincaid Toys insignia— an openmouthed, wide-eyed clown—may not be the sexiest logo to fly at two hundred miles an hour around a superspeedway, but it was a damn good sponsor. And Thunder Jackson would have known that, too.

"I didn't quit, Daddy," she whispered again, almost touching the glistening paint. Unwilling to risk a smudge, she held her fingers a centimeter from the cool metal, imagining the power surge that would sing through the carburetor and make this baby roar to a heart-stopping victory. "Just like you always said, Daddy. Never, never, never quit."

"Actually, Winston Churchill said that." A voice. Deep. Male. Nearby.

Shelby scanned the empty shop.

Then slowly, as if she'd conjured him up, a man rose from the other side of the car. "Unless Winston was your daddy."

"Huh?" Lame, but it was all she could manage in the face of eyes as green as the grass on the front stretch of Daytona. All she could say as she took in sun-streaked hair that fell past his ears and grazed a chiseled jaw. Below that, a white T-shirt molded to a torso that started off wicked, slid right into sinful and braked hard over narrow hips in worn blue jeans.

"Which I highly doubt since Winston's children are..." His eyes glimmered, took a hot lap over her face and body and then returned to meet her gaze. "Quite a bit older than you are."

He straightened to what had to be six feet two, judging by how he dwarfed the race car. "Not to mention," he added, a melodic British accent intensified by the upward curl of generous lips, "there's not a redhead in that whole family."

"Who…?" *Are you?*

"Winston Churchill."

"You are?"

He laughed, and Shelby felt the impact right down to her toes. Which, at the moment, were curled in her boots.

"No relation, I'm afraid. But since we're fellow countrymen, I feel the need to preserve history. To be perfectly honest, the quote was 'Never, never, never give in,' but it's been messed with over the years. And the man who said it was not your daddy."

Actually, it was. But who was she to argue with…perfection?

"It's just an expression." Her voice was husky, her brain stalled. She cleared her throat and seized some missing gray matter. "What are you doing in here?"

He cocked his head and lifted one mighty impressive shoulder. "Checking out the car. Do you like the colors?"

Oh, of *course*. Long hair, foreign accent and just enough beard growth to suggest a distant relationship with a razor. He was the artist. The specialist hired to paint the car.

Although somehow she couldn't imagine the

uptight and virtuous David Kincaid sharing space or business with a man who probably had "bad" tattooed somewhere…good.

"I do like the colors," she assured him. "I like them a lot." And the painter was pretty easy on the eyes, too.

"I think they're atrocious. Too lemon and violet."

Lemon and *violet?* Artistespeak. "Oh, well," she said. "It'll all be one brilliant blur at two hundred miles an hour."

"Let me ask you something."

Anything. Name, rank, phone number.

"Do these little things really go that fast?"

Fahst. Could he be any sexier? "Not at Daytona. That's a plate race."

"I thought it was a car race."

She laughed. "Very funny."

He winked at her. "In any case, I imagine your clown will look especially fetching crossing the finish line under that flag."

He made a word like *fetching* sound so… fetching. Who used that word anymore? "You mean the checkered flag."

"The victory flag."

Adorable. Incredible. Just plain edible. But

the boy did not know racing. "That'd be the one." She stood on her tiptoes to see over the roof. "Still touching up over there?"

He slowly raised his right hand, and a shiny restrictor plate caught the light. "I saw this on the floor and thought it looked intriguing."

"That's one way to describe it." A bane of a racer's existence would be another.

He held the plate over his face, peering at her through the top two holes. "What is it?"

"It's a restrictor plate. That's what makes it a plate race," she explained. "On superspeedways, we have to limit the horsepower."

He lowered the plate and looked appalled. "Why would you do that?"

"It's complicated, but it has to do with safety. You see, if you slide that thing between the carburetor and the intake manifold, you limit the amount of air into the engine, which…" She paused at the amused flicker in his eyes. "You have no idea what an intake manifold is, do you?"

"No, but it sounds hot."

Speaking of hot…

She cleared her throat. Should she tell Painter Boy he was flirting with the co-owner of the race team? She didn't want to scare him off.

"We haven't been introduced," she said.

"No, we haven't." He pinned her with those jade-green eyes, the playful hint of a secret visible enough to send a shiver up her spine.

The shop loudspeaker crackled. "Shelby Jackson, pick up line one."

"But you're being paged."

Oh. So he knew exactly who he was flirting with.

She backed away from the car. "Excuse me," she said, turning to the shop phone on the wall, heat prickling over her neck and a weird, foreign numbness slowing her step.

Unable to resist, she glanced over her shoulder. Sure enough, he still wore a cocky grin, his eyes trained on her with a look that was purely...*sinful*.

She picked up the phone. "'Sup?"

"*'Sup?* What kind of greeting is that for your grandfather?"

"Ernie!" she exclaimed, the familiar rasp of his voice slamming her back to earth. "Are you in the shop?"

"Of course I'm in the shop. I'm in your office. We had a meeting scheduled."

Talk about sinful. Missing a meeting with

her grandfather and business partner was unfor-
givable. "I'm sorry. I got distracted." Big-time.
"Did you see the fifty-three car?" Surely that
was a legitimate excuse for being late.

"Hours ago. Now get on back here before I
die of old age waitin' on ya."

She smiled. "Not likely."

Taking a deep breath, she hung up and
paused before turning around. Should she
make a move? Should she offer her phone
number or take his? Should she act on this
palpable, delicious attraction? So what if he
was a painter and she was a NASCAR team
owner? She hadn't gone on a date in two years,
and he was…

Sinful.

Wouldn't her father give her a nudge to the
ribs? Wouldn't Thunder Jackson whisper in her
ear and say, "Come on, Shelby girl. You only live
once."

"So," she said, still facing the phone on the
wall, "you planning on painting all of our cars?"

She waited a beat, then turned, expecting to
see that provocative tip of his lips, that bedroom
gleam in his eyes.

But the only face that greeted her was the

clown on the hood of the car. Lemon. Violet. And so not sinful.

She uncurled her toes, cursed her moment of female fluttering and hustled off to find Ernie.

HER GRANDFATHER WAS flipping through her phone messages when she entered the office. She paused and sucked in a sigh of exasperation, the usual excuse ringing in her ears.

He means well.

"Ernie?"

He kept reading. "I see no new sponsors have called in the last two days."

She blew out a breath and gave his shoulder a playful punch. "I'm working on it, big guy."

He looked up from the pink slips, snagging her with copper-penny eyes much like her own, only these were minted more than seven decades ago and time had faded them to a dull brown.

"We need money, Shel."

"I know. I know." She slipped behind the desk and dropped into her worn chair and listened for the comfortable, lazy squeak. *Morning, Dad.*

"Been eight years, Shel. When you gonna give that chair a lube job?"

"He doesn't like when you say that, Ernie."

She gave him a sly grin and purposefully rocked, the rhythmic squawk hitting a high note. "You can't quiet Thunder Jackson."

"Lord knows I tried since the day he was born." The older man chuckled, but then his weather-lined skin crinkled into a well-set scowl. "You said you'd be here at seven."

"I didn't think you'd really be here that early." She tapped the mouse to bring her computer screen to life with a twenty-year-old picture of her dad climbing out of a race-torn Ford on the start/finish in Bristol. The year she came back to travel with her father, motherless, eight and scared. That victory was a sign, Daddy had said, that everything would be okay. There would be no more changes. And she'd believed him. "You don't have to get in here so early," she added, looking away from the picture. "I'm handling things."

He grunted, a note of resentment barely hidden in the sound. She almost kicked herself with a work boot. She had to remember not to rub in the fact that he played such a small role in the day-to-day operations of Thunder Racing; running the race team he and her father had started was in his blood.

Without the challenges of the job, Ernie Jackson would be a shell of a man, living in the past. Shelby had to resist the temptation to remind him that she made the most important decisions now. She had to respect that her grandpa needed to run Thunder Racing as much as he needed to eat, breathe and sleep.

"I'm quitting, Shel."

The chair hinge screamed as she jerked toward him. "What?"

"I'm quitting the business."

She stared at him. So much for how well she knew her closest relative.

"Don't look at me like I grew another head, girl. I'm seventy-seven years old." He squished his face into a network of creases so deep that even his wrinkles had wrinkles. "I been on a racetrack or in a garage since I was too young to see over the hood and I been losin' sleep over this team since your daddy was dirt racing. I'm done." His voice softened and he leaned forward. "There's more to life than riding around in circles."

She barely managed to blink. "Where did this come from?"

He crossed his arms over a chest that had

long ago lost its barrel status. "I just want to enjoy my golden years."

He was lying. "Are you sick?"

"Sick of breathin' octane and rubber." He shifted in the chair. "I just want a life without racing is all."

"There's life without racing?" The words were out before she could check herself, earning her a dismal, gruff laugh in response.

"Thunder and me sure failed you, girl, if you really believe that racing is all there is."

"Well, there's the garage. And the pits." She tried to make it sound like a joke. "And the infield."

But he wasn't smiling. "Shelby, you're twenty-eight years old and you work, eat and sleep racing."

She choked a laugh. "And to think I was just about to accuse you of the same crime."

Ernie shook his head, a thin gray lock sliding over his forehead. "And that's fine, honey. I got no issue with that. I just…well, you need to be set up so you're safe and comfortable. We gotta think of the future."

"Right. The future." A future without Ernie was bleak. Lonely. Even a little scary. "Which is why you quitting makes no sense at all."

Ernie pushed that hair away and leaned back on the two legs of the guest chair. She resisted the compulsion to pull his seventy-seven-year-old self to a more secure position.

"Shel, I been givin' this a lot of thought during the off-season," he said slowly. "Before we launch into Daytona next month and the rest of the season, we ought to make a change in our corporate structure."

"I wasn't aware we had a corporate structure." She let out a sober laugh as a little tendril of anxiety tightened her throat. *Change.* Why did she loathe that word? Because every time a major change visited her well-constructed life, it came with pain and loss, that's why. And this one looked headed in the same direction. "Ernie, this is one of the last family-owned teams in NASCAR, not some gargantuan organization with six hundred employees and their own wind-tunnel simulator. What could we possibly change except who's responsible for picking up the donuts on Monday morning?"

There was no humor in his eyes. "You know as well as I do that if we don't upgrade that small-potato mind-set we'll never be in NASCAR NEXTEL Cup racing next year, let alone thrive into the next decade. We got one year left with our sponsors, and after that, honey, we're gonna be field fillers if we're lucky."

"Ernie, I'm working on that," she said, her smile fading as the seriousness of what he was saying hit her. "Or have you forgotten that I convinced Kincaid Toys to sponsor a second Thunder car and I signed Clayton Slater to drive it for us? Now we have *two* cars and two drivers and two major sponsors. That's plenty secure and..." She shifted in her seat and set her jaw. "I don't want to get any bigger than that."

"Don't worry. We're a far cry from the four cars and drivers, the mountains of money and the international corporate sponsorships that the big teams have."

She shoved the desk with both hands, rolling her chair back with a grunt of disgust. "Well, good for them, Ernie. Thunder Racing isn't ever going to be a race team like that. We're real. We're old-school. We race like stock-car racing was meant to be, not like some giant operation with...with..." She waved a frustrated hand. "That just wasn't what Daddy wanted, and you know it."

His expression turned sympathetic. "Why are you fighting it so hard, Shel? The sport has changed, even since Thunder died. It's all different now. The whole world knows what NASCAR racin' is. We're darn near more popular than football, for cryin' out loud."

"And why is that a good thing?" she demanded.

"Don't matter if it is or not," he said quietly. "But it's the way of our world, and your father isn't around to let us know if he likes it or not. And if we don't get on that track and trade some paint with the big boys, we might as well close the doors now. Meantime, I'm retiring after this season, that gives me this year to get you set up for the future."

She clenched her jaw. "Retiring is your prerogative, Ernie."

"But I'm not leaving this place until I know you are set up to be competitive and I don't think a four-race season of filling the field is competitive. I want you racin' with the real teams, makin' the Chase, maybe winnin' a Cup. Then I can sleep at night." He slumped in his chair, suddenly looking drained.

Had she been so caught up in fighting the fight that she'd failed to notice Ernie getting older before her very eyes? Could she do this without him? The question sent blood pumping in her ears, but beyond that everything seemed unnaturally quiet.

After a few beats, she finally leaned forward on her elbows. "So you want to be a silent partner, Ernie?" She didn't like it, but he'd always be there to offer advice. Well, maybe not *always*. "I can live with that."

The shake of his head was so slight it was nearly imperceptible.

"You want me to buy you out?" Still not the end of the world. She'd figure out a way. She always did. "Let's talk numbers then."

"No."

She frowned at him. "No what?"

"No, I'm not selling to you. I found a buyer for my half of the business."

For a moment that blood in her ears just stopped cold. "Excuse me?"

"I have a plan, Shel, and I want you to hear me out before you start stompin' your boots and gettin' all redheaded tempery."

But she couldn't stomp. Her legs were numb. "Who?"

"Well, it's not just who…." He repositioned himself and took a deep breath. "It's what he is."

What he was? Oh, she didn't like the sound of that.

"Before I tell you, I want you to think—"

"I don't want to think. I want to know. Who is it?"

"Think about the future, Shel." His gaze shifted to the image of Thunder on her computer screen. "Instead of the past."

She leaned forward, slowly enough to let Thunder's chair moan, low and plaintive. "Ernie, if you want to sell out to some mammoth corporation with a bunch of suits in a boardroom more concerned about household impressions than horsepower, I'll never go along with it."

"I'm not," he said, his eyes lighting. "Really, I'm not. And I swear to you I won't do anything without your one hundred per cent agreement. You gotta buy into this, just like I have."

Her shoulders dropped and she released a breath she hadn't realized she was holding. That blood thumping had stopped in her head. Replaced by…nothing. The sound of relief, she imagined. "Then who?"

"I met someone. Someone who can bring us international attention, someone who can bring fresh ideas and new blood, someone who has an uncanny understanding of how to draw people in and make them want to root for you."

Only half her brain was taking in his "someone" speech. The other half was stuck on the silence. Holding up one hand, she stood, frowning, listening. "Just a sec, Ernie. Do you hear that?"

"I don't hear a thing," he said. "But then, I'm damn near deaf."

"No. You're right. You don't hear a thing." She closed her eyes and focused on the sound of silence in the air. "No engines, no tools, no work being done." She glanced toward the shop. "It's perfectly quiet out there."

He stood slowly, his signature scowl firmly in place. "What's going on?"

Wordlessly they both walked to the door, down the hall and into the cavernous—and empty—shop.

"Do you think the new hauler was delivered early?" she asked. "It's not due here till ten or so."

An array of tools and equipment was spread on the shiny white floor as though they'd been dropped. Impossible.

"I don't hear anything from the engine area either," she noted to Ernie.

He pointed to where the wall of garage doors stood wide-open. As soon as he did, the first of the North Carolina winter chill wafted over Shelby. Ernie rounded an open Craftsman tool chest, and Shelby nearly hurdled over it. Something was wrong.

She paused at a loud shout, followed by what sounded like applause. Applause?

Just beyond the open doors, at least thirty Thunder employees gathered in a large circle among nearly melted snowbanks, white clouds of late-January air puffing from everyone's mouth as they hollered and screamed and cheered.

Shelby took a few steps outside, peering to see between the bodies. Was someone fighting? Performing? What was going on?

She glanced at Ernie and caught a funny, knowing expression in his eyes. "What?" she asked.

He just lifted his eyebrows but didn't speak.

She marched toward the crowd, her boots crunching on the frozen grass. Just as she approached, a black-and-white ball shot in the air and two people stepped aside, forming a break and giving her a clear shot of a man in the middle of the circle.

Shelby stared, slack-jawed, wide-eyed and only vaguely aware that her heart slid around her chest and hit her ribs like a rear quarter panel slamming into the wall.

It was him. The painter. He was surrounded by a crowd and...*kicking a soccer ball?*

As though he sensed her there, he spun around and locked those green eyes on her, flipping a lock of long, blond hair off his face. Just as the soccer ball came plummeting back to earth, he whacked it with his knee, shooting it skyward again and eliciting a delighted cheer from the crowd.

He never took his eyes off her.

Behind her, Ernie's hands tightened on Shelby's shoulders as he pulled her just a little closer. "Do you recognize him?" he asked.

She blinked. "The guy who painted the car?"

Ernie snorted. "Not hardly. That's Mick Churchill, the most famous soccer player on the globe. That man is the most popular, beloved athlete in the universe."

Really. "I never heard of him," she murmured.

"Get your head out of the hood, girl. He's an international icon. A media magnet. A household name in every home in Europe, South

America and beyond. That man is a corporate sponsor's dream."

Why did Ernie know so much about some soccer star?

The blood started singing in her head again. Oh, no. No, no...*no.*

"And that man, Shel, is going to be the new co-owner of Thunder Racing."

Slowly Shelby turned to burn her grandfather with an incredulous stare. "You have got to be kidding."

But he looked so pleased she thought he'd do a little jig. "Isn't this great?"

"Great? Are you serious?"

"Oh, I'm serious." He looked past her, back to the man who stood at the center of the circle—and threatened the center of her universe. "Mick Churchill is the answer to our prayers."

She turned back just in time to see him catapult the ball over the treetops again, laughing easily as the applause and cheers rose as high as the ball.

His muscular body moved with fluid grace. She narrowed her eyes in distaste, but her body betrayed her with a response that was the polar opposite of distaste.

The answer to their prayers? "I guess that depends on what you're praying for, Ernie."

"I was praying for a miracle," he said quietly. "And then I met Mick."

"Well, I've never heard of him," she repeated, as though that would negate everything Ernie had just said.

"Then you're the only one on the planet," Ernie said. "Trust me, this man will bring worldwide interest to Thunder Racing and sponsors with endless pockets and oodles of cash."

Cash again. Resentment rocked her as the crowd oohed loudly. She shook her head in dismay. "He doesn't know squat about racing," she said, unable to take her eyes off him.

"He knows sports." Ernie squeezed her shoulders as if he could transfer his excitement to her. "He knows the media. He's buying a NASCAR team, and we want it to be ours."

They did? She flinched out of his touch and glared at him. "He doesn't know a restrictor plate from a...a...a dinner plate!"

"Don't matter." Ernie looked past her, then his gaze followed the upward path of a flying soccer ball. "I think he's perfect."

Slowly Shelby turned back to find Mick Churchill staring at her.

Oh, he was perfect all right. Perfect for flirting. Perfect for heartache and sin and trouble. Perfect for a whole host of things that could bring a woman to her knees or flat on her back, but so not perfect for Thunder Racing.

She pivoted on one foot and seared her grandfather with her most obstinate gaze. "No way. Not happening. Forget about it."

He tapped her chin and chuckled. "That's what I love about you, Shel. You're as open-minded as your daddy. But you'll come around."

Oh, no, she wouldn't.

* * * * *

Mick is determined to change Shelby's mind...any way he can! Find out how in THUNDERSTRUCK *by Roxanne St. Claire, on sale in February 2007 for a limited time. See next page for a valuable coupon.*

Blood pumping
Pulses accelerating

Falling in love can be
a blur...especially at

180 mph!

So if you crave the thrill
of the chase—on and off
the track—you'll love

THUNDERSTRUCK
by Roxanne St. Claire

On sale February 2007.

www.GetYourHeartRacing.com

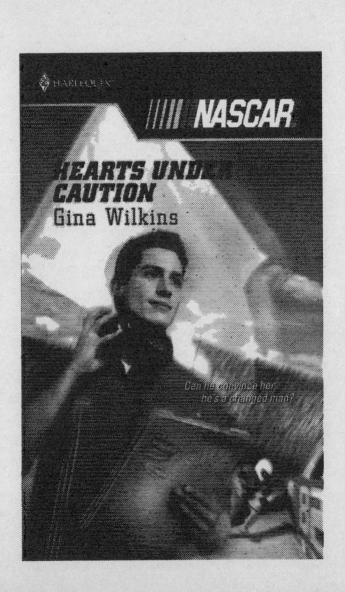

HARLEQUIN

|||||| NASCAR

HEARTS UNDER CAUTION
Gina Wilkins

Can he convince her he's a changed man?

CHAPTER ONE

THE MOONLIT NIGHT WAS STILL, the late July temperature warm but comfortable as Lisa Woodrow sat on a concrete bench in her mother's North Carolina garden. Heavy perfumes from many varieties of roses tickled her nose and carried her back to her past. As she had so often in those blissfully naive and hopelessly romantic younger days, she found herself thinking of Wade McClellan....

A rustling in a far corner of the large garden brought her abruptly back to the present. Every nerve ending in her body on sudden alert, she sat up straight, straining her ears. When the sound wasn't repeated, she let out the breath she'd been holding and tried to relax, assuring herself that there was nothing to fear here.

She had plenty of reason to be on edge after the events of the past week. It didn't soothe her frazzled nerves to know that Wade was inside her parents' house, meeting with her father and a few other top members of the Woodrow Racing team.

Since team owner Ernest "Woody" Woodrow had undergone a full hip replacement ten days earlier, limiting his movements for a few weeks, the majority of his meetings had taken place here, in his home office. His highest-ranking team members had arrived right after dinner on this Monday evening to discuss the race week ahead. Wade had been the first of those arrivals.

It had been obvious that he hadn't known Lisa was there, since she'd flown in only a few hours earlier, but he had recovered quickly from his surprise. He'd greeted her with the same polite distance he'd displayed on the few other occasions when they'd crossed paths over the last six years. She'd responded in the same cool manner—and had made her escape at the very first available opportunity.

It was the first time she'd seen him in over a year. He looked tired, she thought. Too thin. His tanned skin was drawn a little too tightly over the carved planes of his face. His brown eyes were shadowed, the sun-creases at the corners more deeply defined than she remembered. And there was now a touch of gray at the temples of his functionally short, pecan-brown hair.

Yet even as she acknowledged the signs that he hadn't changed his fiercely workaholic habits, her heart pounded so hard in her chest that she'd been afraid he could hear it over her cool, carefully disinterested voice. After almost six years and a whole new life, one would think she'd have gotten over the sight of him by now.

The rustling came again.

It brought Lisa to her feet. Poised for flight, she held her breath, trying to hear over her hammering pulse. She'd thought the sound came from behind her and to the left, but was she wrong? Had it been between her and the safety of the house?

No. Definitely behind her.

Maybe it was a cat, or some other small, nocturnal animal. Maybe nothing but overwrought imagination. She didn't stick around to find out. She bolted, heading straight for the house, making no effort to be quiet.

When she slammed into a solid and unmistakably male body, she reacted on pure instinct, striking out. She opened her mouth to scream.

"Lisa!" Wade's voice cut through her moment of panic, turning the budding shriek into a squeak of surprise. His hands fell on her shoulders, steadying them both and making her realize how close she'd come to flattening him. "What's wrong? Are you okay?"

Her breath was still coming out too audibly, a combination of her former fear and now awareness of Wade standing so close to her, holding her. She took a quick step backward, dislodging his hands.

He let his arms fall to his sides, but his too-sharp gaze remained on her face. "What's wrong?" he repeated.

She took a moment to regain control. She could barely see him in the diffused garden lighting, but she knew her own face was more visible to him since there was a pole lamp directly behind him, illuminating her while keeping him in the shadows.

"I thought I heard someone moving around in the garden," she said when she was sure her voice would come out relatively steady. "Watching me."

His head lifted as if he'd just caught scent of a predator. Looking from side to side, he asked, "Where?"

She started to point in the direction she'd thought the noise had come from, but then stopped and shook her head. "I'm not sure. If anyone was there, he'd be gone by now anyway."

"You know it's unlikely anyone was in the garden with you. The property is fully fenced and your dad has top of the line security equipment. It wouldn't be easy for anyone to get in nor to get back out unnoticed."

"Yes, I know." But the hesitancy she heard in her response probably let him know she wasn't entirely reassured. To distract him, she asked, "What are you doing out here? Were you looking for me?"

"Yeah. I was."

Even though she had asked, his answer still surprised her. "Why?"

"I got the impression that something was bothering you. Something more than me being here, I mean. I wanted to see if there's anything I can do."

She supposed she shouldn't be so taken aback that he'd seen too much during their brief interaction earlier. Wade had always read her too well— with a few very painful exceptions. "I'm okay."

"Are you sure? Because you look kind of shaky."

What pride she retained after being caught by Wade on the verge of a full-blown panic attack kicked into full force. She lifted her chin. "I'm fine, Wade. I guess I'm just tired. It's my first real vacation in almost three years. I hadn't realized quite how much I needed one. Now, if you'll excuse me, I think I'll head inside, maybe turn in early tonight."

"Lisa—"

Ignoring the hand he held out to detain her, she stepped around him and moved resolutely toward her parents' house. "Good night, Wade," she said over her shoulder without looking back.

It was no surprise that he didn't respond.

WADE WAS BACK THE NEXT MORNING. Lisa hadn't seen him when he arrived, but her mother told her that he was meeting with Woody and the other three Woodrow Racing crew chiefs in Woody's office. Sitting in the solarium before noon, surrounded by her mother's pampered and beloved flowering plants, Lisa merely shrugged when her mother asked her how she felt about Wade being around so much during her visit.

"He isn't usually here at the house," Ellen

added a bit anxiously. "You know, your father usually prefers not to do business at home. But since his surgery, it's easier for the meetings to be held here."

"I understand—and it's fine, Mom. I certainly don't want to interfere with Dad's business meetings just because I'm here for a visit. And as for Wade, you know he and I have seen each other several times during the past few years. It's not a problem."

"It can't be comfortable for you, having your ex-fiancé in the house," Ellen fretted.

Smiling, Lisa shook her head. "It's not a problem," she repeated. "My ex-fiancé still works for my father. It's a given that he and I will run into each other at times. Besides, it isn't as if Wade and I had a bitter breakup. It was all very amicable, remember? We've remained friendly."

She didn't go so far as to say they were still friends. She wasn't sure she and Wade had ever been friends, even when they were lovers. He hadn't let her get to know him that well.

Virginia Cooper, who had been employed by the family since Lisa was barely out of diapers, appeared in the doorway with a smile to announce that lunch was ready. There had been a time when Virginia had only worked a couple of days a week doing the laundry and the heavy cleaning, but since Ellen had taken ill a year ago, she came in every day to cook and run the household.

Ellen had protested at first, but Lisa suspected that she was secretly grateful for the extra help. Now she spent her days caring for her flowers, fussing over her husband and resting quite a bit.

Lisa's steps faltered a little when she saw Wade waiting with her father in the breakfast nook where the informal luncheon was to be served. He gave her a rather stiff nod of greeting.

"Wade and I aren't quite through with our business today," Woody announced gruffly. "He's going to be joining us for lunch and then we'll finish up afterward. I'm sure that's okay with you ladies?"

Though he'd posed it as a question, it was obvious that Woody expected no protests from his wife or daughter. It wasn't that he was oblivious to the awkwardness inherent in the situation, Lisa thought in resignation. It was just that he didn't have time for old dramas when he had business to discuss.

As much as he cared for his family, business always came first for her father. It was a fact Lisa had accepted a very long time ago.

As was their usual habit, her parents sat at opposite ends of the small breakfast table, so that Lisa and Wade faced each other from the sides. Ellen didn't believe in long, stilted silences at her table, so she kicked off the conversation as they began to eat the cold chicken salad, fresh asparagus spears and fruit compote that Virginia had served for a light lunch.

"How have you been, Wade?" she asked cordially. "Have you fully recovered from that flu bug you picked up a few weeks ago?"

So that was why he still looked a bit worn, Lisa thought, glancing at the lines around his mouth. She didn't remember Wade ever being sick when she was involved with him; he said he didn't have time to deal with germs.

"Yes, ma'am, I'm feeling fine now," he said with the same deference he had always displayed toward his boss's wife. "Thank you for asking."

"Took him down pretty hard," Woody said to Lisa. "He missed three days of work that week. Made it to the racetrack, though."

"Of course he did," she murmured without looking at Wade. He'd have to be on his deathbed to miss a race, she thought. And she wouldn't guarantee even then that he wouldn't take the risk of just dropping dead in the pits, doing what he loved more than anything—or anyone—in the world.

"Lisa, do you have any interesting stories to tell us about your job in Chicago?" her mother asked determinedly. "Any exciting cases lately?"

Other than the case that had sent her running to North Carolina out of fear for her very life? "Not really," she said with a bland smile. "Just the usual."

She sensed Wade's intense gaze on her face. It took an effort for her to keep her smile intact.

"Your mother got all nervous last week because she decided your life was just like one of those mystery novels she's always reading," Woody said with an indulgent shake of his head.

Looking a little sheepish, Ellen smiled. "I was reading a story about a prosecutor who was stalked by the vengeful relative of a criminal she'd put away," she explained. "It was set in L.A., but I couldn't help but think about you.

Chicago is such a dangerous city and you deal with so many unsavory people in your job."

Lisa felt the corners of her smile tremble, but she forced her lips to behave. "Chicago's not as bad as you make it sound, Mom. And my life really isn't all that dramatic."

She wasn't exactly lying, she assured herself. Her job usually wasn't dangerous. But how coincidental was it that her mother had read that book so recently? Just talking about it made the color fade from her mom's face.

She shouldn't have come here, Lisa thought guiltily. She should have taken her boss's suggestion to find someplace safe and secluded to vacation for a few weeks, keeping her problems far away from her parents, who had enough to worry about right now. But for some reason she'd found herself wanting to come home, even though she had promised herself she wouldn't tell her family the real purpose behind the extended visit.

Obviously, she hadn't thought her decision through. She certainly hadn't planned to be lunching with Wade only a day after her arrival.

"You must be really excited about the way this season is going," she said brightly to her father, hoping no one would see any significance in the jarringly sudden change of topic. "Two of your drivers sitting in the top ten points positions and a third driver not far behind. That would really be something if three of your four teams ended up in the Chase at the end, wouldn't it?"

Both her dad and Wade looked at her oddly, as if they were surprised that she knew where the Woodrow Racing drivers stood in points coming up on the twentieth race of the thirty-sixth race season. Maybe they were startled that she even knew that only the top ten points leaders and those drivers within 400 points of first place were eligible to race for the NASCAR NEXTEL Cup during the last ten races of the season, a system referred to as the Chase for the Championship.

She supposed she shouldn't be surprised by *their* surprise. Since her father had been so determined to keep his family and work life separate, she had been kept well away from the racing world in her youth, forced to learn about the sport by watching televised race coverage like the average fan.

"Er, yeah," Woody said awkwardly. "We're doing real good."

"Mom said you and Wade have been meeting about hiring a new engineer. How's the search going?"

"Good," her father said with a curt nod. "Got it narrowed down to just a few. We'll talk about it some more after lunch. This salad's good, Virginia. I like the almonds in it."

Having just approached the table with a pitcher of iced tea to refill their glasses, the housekeeper beamed. "I'm glad you like it, Mr. Woody. Does anyone need anything else before I go?"

When everyone assured her that nothing else was needed, Virginia told them to enjoy their meals and to leave their dishes when they were finished. She bustled away to finish her chores, leaving a silence in her wake that even Ellen didn't seem to know how to fill as they finished their lunches.

WADE FINISHED HIS BUSINESS with Woody an hour and a half after they'd returned to Woody's office after lunch. Leaving Woody already engrossed in a conference call with a potential sponsor, he made his way through the house toward the front door, needing no escort.

The house was quiet; he suspected that Ellen was napping, as was her habit in the afternoons since she'd been ill. He didn't know where Lisa was—not that he was looking, he assured himself.

He had his answer when he passed the open doorway of the front salon, just off the entryway. It was a room the family used as a library. Lisa was inside, her back turned toward him as she stood in front of a filled bookcase, looking through her mother's treasured collection of mystery novels.

Wade paused, considered moving on without speaking but then changed his mind. He was suddenly reminded of the conversation they'd had at lunch, when Ellen had told them about the book she'd recently read. Something about a prosecutor being targeted by a killer. Ellen had looked sheepish about taking the tale too seriously and being worried for her daughter's sake. But it was Lisa's expression he remembered most vividly.

She hadn't laughed off her mother's concerns. She had made some offhand remark about not confusing fact with fiction—but then she'd quickly changed the subject. And he would have sworn she'd lost a couple of shades of color from her face—which had already been pale.

He had suspected since he'd first seen her yesterday that something was going on with Lisa. Something she wasn't telling her family. And even though it was absolutely none of his business, he couldn't help but feel that he should offer his assistance, if she needed it. Though he doubted there was anything he could do for her—or that she would accept his help, regardless.

Making a sudden decision, he moved forward. "Lisa?"

She gasped and jumped half a foot, whirling around as if she'd heard a gun cock behind her.

"Oh," she said, her voice unsteady. "Wade. You startled me."

"Sorry." He studied her face, convinced now that he'd been right about something shady going on with her. "What's up?"

"I was just looking for something to read."

He shook his head impatiently. "You've taken

a month's vacation from your job. You've lost weight. You jump halfway out of your shoes at the slightest sound. Maybe your mother accepts your explanation that you've just been working too hard and need a break, but that doesn't cut it with me. Your dad thinks there's more to it, too."

"Sounds like my father's been talking too much," she grumbled.

"He's worried about you. He thinks the job's too much for you to handle."

"My father can't understand why I'd want to be a prosecutor when I could stay here and let him take care of me. Or find some other man to take care of me," she added a bit pointedly. "But I love my job. And I am quite capable of handling it just fine, thank you."

"I never doubted it," Wade muttered, hearing the resignation in his own voice. "But you're sure there isn't something bothering you? Nothing I can do to help? Even if it's just to serve as a sounding board. I'm available now for a couple of hours."

She looked ready to brush him off again. But then she bit her lip, looked toward the doorway and nervously tucked a lock of her straight blond hair behind her ear.

"Lees?" he said more gently, using her old nickname for the first time in almost six years. "Let me help."

She sighed deeply. "I shouldn't have come here. I thought it would be safe for a few weeks and that my parents would be safe with me here. Now…now I'm questioning the wisdom of that decision."

"Okay, now you're just creeping me out," he said bluntly, reaching out to lay his hand on her shoulder. "Tell me what's going on."

"It's going to take a while," she said after another long pause. "And I'd rather my parents didn't hear what I have to say. Not yet, anyway."

He nodded, both relieved that she seemed willing to talk and unnerved by what little she had already said. "Then we need to go where we can talk in private. Want to have a drink with me somewhere?"

She hesitated only another moment, then nodded. "Yes. To be honest, I would be grateful for your advice."

Though he was a bit surprised that she'd accepted his invitation, he didn't let it show. Over the past few years he'd gotten very good

at hiding his emotions from Lisa, he thought
wryly. Just as he did from everyone else.

THE COFFEE SHOP WADE TOOK HER to was small.
Quiet on a Tuesday afternoon. Sitting in a cozy
booth at the back with Lisa, Wade knew he'd
been recognized by some of the other custom-
ers, but they gave him his privacy. Perhaps they
sensed that he was in no mood for socializing.

Her parents had been startled, to say the least,
when Lisa had told them that she and Wade
were going out for a while. It had been obvious
that they hadn't expected her to spend any time
alone with her ex-fiancé during her visit. And
just as obvious that her mother wasn't overly en-
thusiastic about her doing so today.

Wade couldn't say he thought this was a brilliant idea, either. He didn't want to be reminded
of those earlier days with Lisa, nor of the painful
end to their relationship. But he still remembered
all too clearly the look on her face when she'd
run straight into his arms in her mother's garden
last night. Not to mention the way she'd jumped
when he'd simply said her name in the library.

Something was seriously wrong in her life.
He had looked into her smoky green eyes and

had seen something he'd never seen in Lisa Woodrow before. Fear.

Because it was late in the afternoon, Lisa ordered a decaf latte. Wade ordered coffee. Black and real. He was usually too tired by the time he crawled into bed for caffeine to keep him awake, no matter how much he consumed during the day.

"Now tell me what's going on," he said when they had their drinks in front of them.

He hadn't meant the request to sound so much like a command. He blamed his curt tone on his uneasiness about her, but he knew Lisa didn't respond well to being given orders. Especially from him. He tried to soften his expression. "Please."

Predictably, she had bristled a little but he'd managed to appease her. She nodded, tucked a lock of hair behind her ear, then gazed into her coffee mug for a moment before saying, "I might have made a mistake coming here."

"Here? With me? Or here, to your parents' house?"

"Both," she said, making a face. "But specifically, I was talking about my parents' house."

As a crew chief, Wade was often forced to

hide his feelings. No matter how bad things got during a race, he had to stay upbeat and optimistic, keeping his driver and team calm and focused, making them all believe he had everything under control. His owner, the sponsors, the media, the fans—no one could tell by his demeanor when things weren't going well with the team. When he was worried or discouraged or stressed.

They called him "Ice." A nickname he tolerated because he'd worked hard to earn it.

Never was he more hard-pressed to hide his feelings than when he was around Lisa. Even after six years, all it took was a little wrinkle of her nose to make his heart stutter. Damn, she was even more beautiful now than she'd been as the girl who had once loved him.

"Maybe you'd better start from the beginning," he said, and this time he didn't care if he sounded too bossy. It was better than letting her see that she still affected him entirely too deeply.

"I know you think I'm home on vacation. But actually, I took a leave of absence because my boss insisted on it," she admitted grudgingly. "And I came home to North Carolina because it was either that or go into protective custody back in Chicago. You see, someone there is trying to kill me."

* * * * *

The only man Lisa can trust with her life is the one she doesn't dare trust with her heart...
Look for HEARTS UNDER CAUTION by Gina Wilkins, on sale in February 2007 for a limited time. See next page for a valuable coupon.

Blood pumping
Pulses accelerating

Falling in love can be a blur...especially at **180 mph!**

So if you crave the thrill of the chase—on and off the track—you'll love **HEARTS UNDER CAUTION** by Gina Wilkins

On sale February 2007.

www.GetYourHeartRacing.com

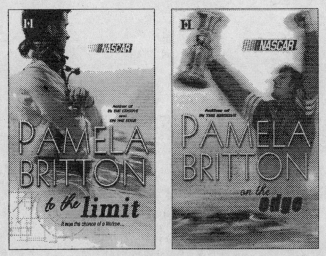

Want to know more?
SIGN UP TODAY!

FREE

INSIDE *Romance*

QUARTERLY NEWSLETTER

Your complete guide to
Harlequin and Silhouette books.

✔ It's absolutely FREE! NO purchase necessary.

✔ Valuable coupons.

✔ Special excerpts and previews.

✔ No hassle—mailed directly to your door.

- -

SIGN ME UP TO RECEIVE *INSIDE ROMANCE* ABSOLUTELY FREE

(Please print clearly)

Name

Address

City/Town   State/Province   Zip/Postal Code

(098 KKN EJL9)   **Sign up online: www.eHarlequin.com/insideromance**

<u>OR</u> mail this form to:
In the U.S.A.: Inside Romance, P.O. Box 9057, Buffalo, NY 14269-9057
In Canada: Inside Romance, P.O. Box 622, Fort Erie, ON L2A 5X3

IRNSAMP07   ® and ™ are trademarks owned and used by the trademark owner and/or its licensee.